FROM THE
BOOK COLLECTION OF:

THE MUSEUM OF ME

'Give me a museum and I'll fill it.'

Pablo Picasso

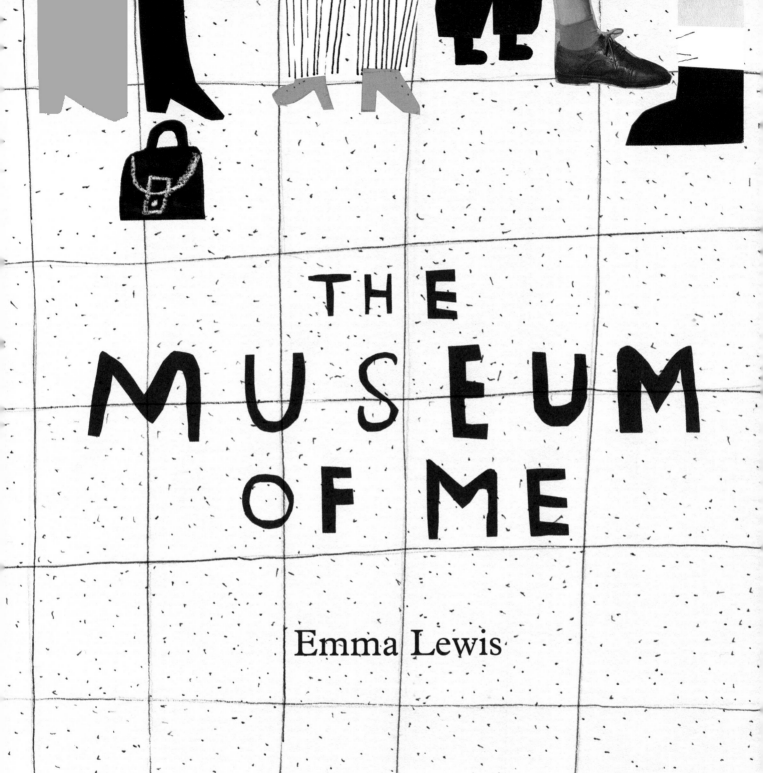

THE MUSEUM OF ME

Emma Lewis

TATE PUBLISHING

Everyone says
I'm going to love
the museums.

Museums are big buildings filled with the oldest and oddest things from all around the world.

And
there are
lots of
them!

This place
is enormous!

It's the
Museum of
Ancient
Artefacts.

The things inside are *thousands* of years old and from *thousands* of miles away

and they all
ended up here!

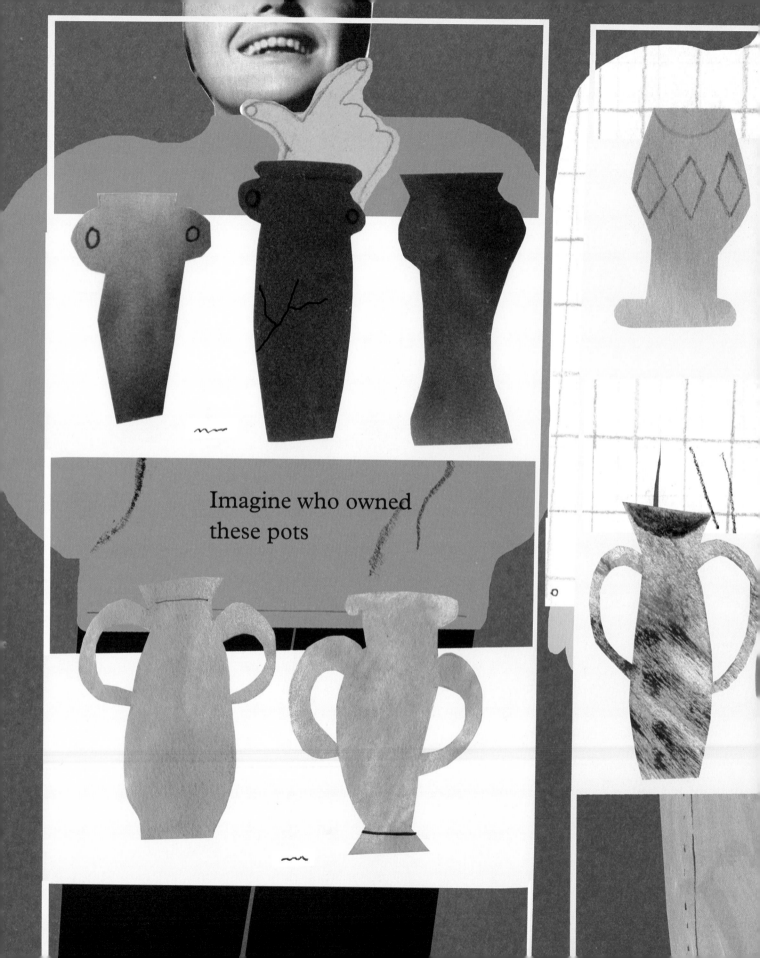

Imagine who owned
these pots

and this cup

or these animals.
Just like the ones in
my toy box!

In the Museum
of Natural History
there are giant bugs
and peculiar beasts.

Rooms of
strange birds
I've never
seen before…

BiRDS

HORNBILLS AND TOUCANS

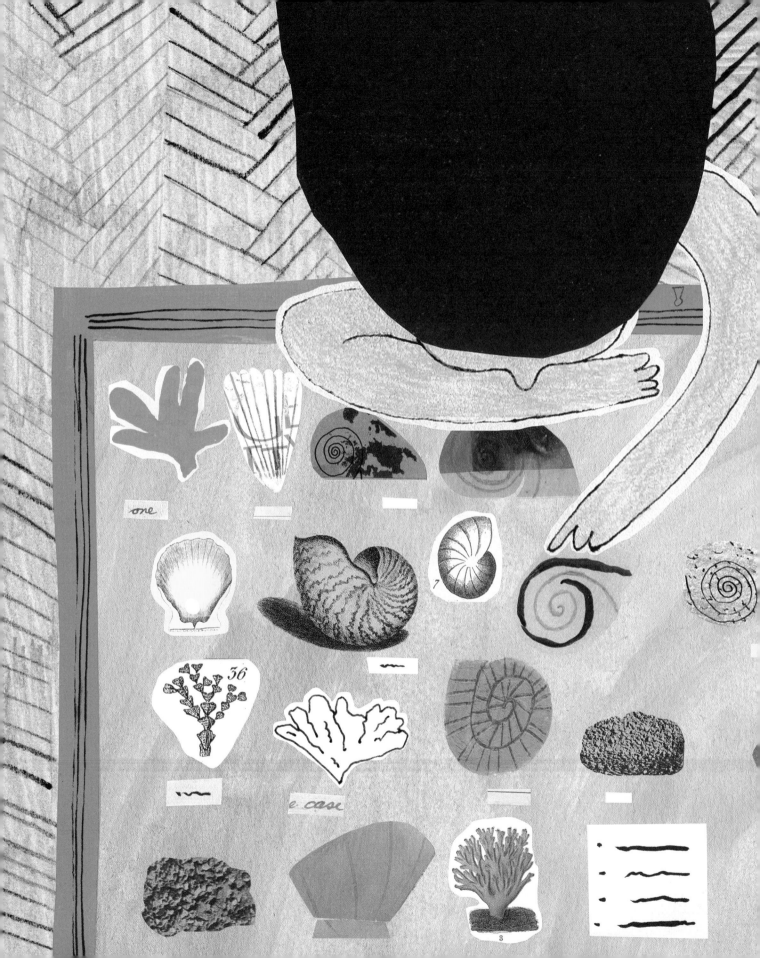

one

36

e case

3

And treasures
found deep
underground and
far out at sea,
brought back by
fearless
explorers!

But this
is a collection
that's not
ancient or wild.

The Museum
of Art is
neither of
those!

And you know,
not all museums
are in big
buildings…

menu

This one's outside.

A museum in a garden.

There are spikey palms
and feathery leaves
and flower heads as big as my own!

A growing collection.

Museums don't have to be old at all!

The Space
Museum has
all sorts of
new things.

What kinds of museums do they have up there?

An endless number, an infinity to visit!

But guess which collection
is still left to see?

One that's
full of my
favourite things.

The museum
I know best.

The Museum of Me!

What do you like to collect?

What's on display
in your own museum?

What other kinds of museums
can you visit?

Can you invent some new ones?

Who do you think the ancient toy animals belonged to?

Can you draw some more here?

Which is your favourite picture from the Museum of Art?

Can you draw some paintings here
to make your own gallery?

For Mum and Dad

Special thanks to Anna, Alice, Angela and Lizzie

First published 2016 by order of the Tate Trustees
by Tate Publishing, a division of Tate Enterprises Ltd,
Millbank, London SW1P 4RG

www.tate.org.uk/publishing

A catalogue record for this book is available from the British Library

ISBN 978-1-84976-414-8

Distributed in the United States and Canada by ABRAMS, New York

Library of Congress Control Number applied for

Designed by Lizzie Ballantyne
Colour reproduction by Evergreen Colour Management Co. Ltd
Printed in China by Toppan Leefung Printing Ltd

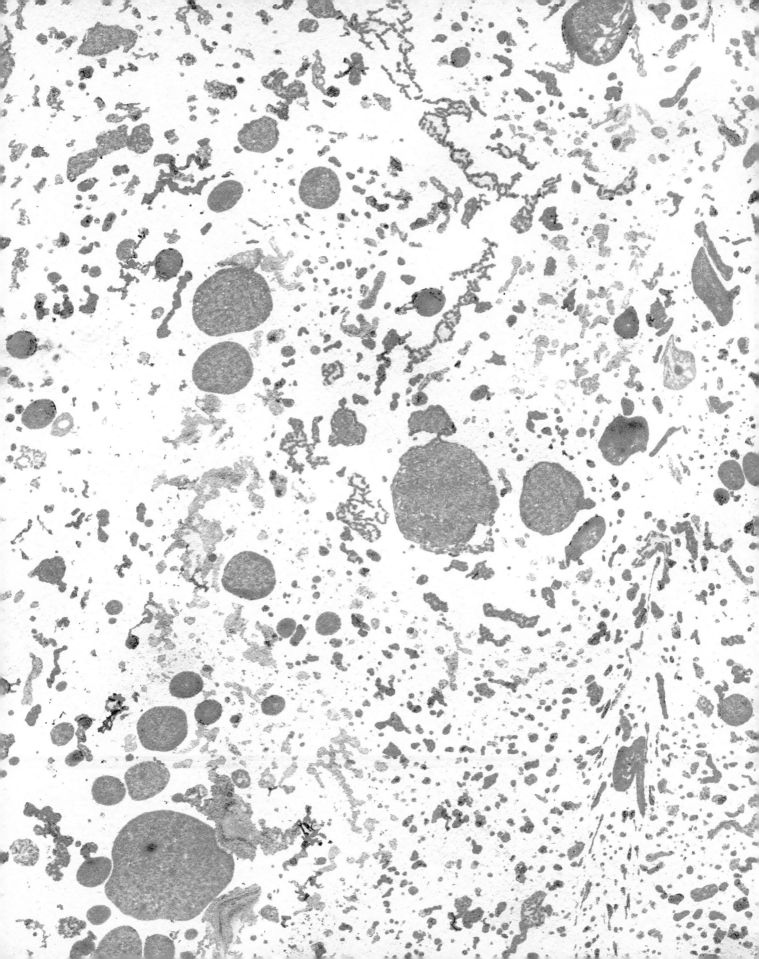